PLACES AND PEOPLE

Japan

Vincent Bunce

Franklin Watts
A Division of Grolier Publishing
New York • London • Hong Kong • Sydney
Danbury, Connecticut

© 1994 Watts Books

First American Edition © 1994 by Franklin Watts
A Division of Grolier Publishing
Sherman Turnpike
Danbury, Connecticut 06816

10 9 8 7 6 5 4 3 2

Library of Congress Cataloging-in-Publication Data

Bunce, Vincent J.
    Japan / Vincent Bunce
        p.   cm. — (Places and people)
    Summary: Examines how Japan's geography influenced its social,
    economic, and political structure.
    Includes index.
    ISBN 0-531-14270-1
    1. Japan-Civilization—Juvenile literature.   2. Human geography-
Japan—Juvenile literature.   [1. Japan-Civilization.   2. Human
geography.] 1. Title.   II. Series: Places and people (New York, N.Y.)
    DS821.B699   1994
    952 - dc20   93-20426
                                      CIP AC

First paperback edition published
in 1996 by Franklin Watts

ISBN 0-531-15293-6

Series consultants: Anna Sanderman
                        Chris Durbin
Editor: Jane Walker
Design: Ron Kamen, Green Door Design Ltd
Cover design: Mike Davis
Maps: Visual Image
      Hayward Art Group
Additional artwork: Hayward Art Group
                      Visual Image
Cover artwork: Raymond Turvey
Fact checking: Simone K. Lefolii
Picture research: Alison Renwick

Cover photographs: top, Geisha girl performong tea ceremony (Bruce
Coleman Ltd / J.T.Wright); middle, Ginza district of Tokyo (Bruce Coleman Ltd / N.Myers);
bottom, robotic testing at factory in Kitakyushu (Jim Holmes).

Photographic credits (t = top, m = middle, b = bottom): Vincent Bunce 23; J.Allan Cash 22(t);
Bruce Coleman Ltd 27(m); Mary Evans Picture Library 22(b); 23(t); Eye Ubiquitous 5(t),
11 Trisha Rafferty, 25(b) R.Haynes; Fujifotos / Andes Press Agency 8, 9, 14, 17(t), 19(t), 20,
27(t, b), 29; Robert Harding 4, 7(m), (b) Gavin Hellier, 17(b) Paolo Koch, 19(b) Michael Jenner;
J.Holmes 7(t), 13(t, b), 25(t); Frank Spooner Pictures 15; TRIP 5(b) Anne Crabbe, 13(m) Peter Ranter.

Printed in Belgium

Contents

4 | *A*n island superpower

6 | *T*he land and the climate

8 | *A* hazardous land

10 | *C*rowded cities, empty countryside

12 | *F*ood, farming, and fishing

14 | *R*esources and energy

16 | *C*ars, cameras, and chips

18 | *G*etting around

20 | *T*rading the world

22 | *F*rom isolation to economic superpower

24 | *M*etropolis Japan

26 | *E*nvironment under threat

28 | *P*ower in the Pacific

30 | *D*atabank

31 | *G*lossary

32 | *I*ndex

An island superpower

Japan is made up of a group of around 3,900 islands that lie just off the east coast of North and South Korea and the Russian Federation. It is one of the world's greatest economic superpowers. Japan produces more cars and cameras than any other country, and is the world's second highest producer of television sets, after China. A quick look around your home, or the local stores, will show you what a large number of everyday items are made in Japan.

The Japanese economy is the second largest in the world (after the United States). Japanese goods can be found throughout the world, and Japanese companies have spread to new locations across Europe and the United States. All this adds up to a huge achievement for a tiny island nation that was in ruins at the end of World War II, almost 50 years ago, and which has few natural resources of its own.

Japan's small land area means that it does not appear in a list of the world's 50 largest nations. However, its islands stretch more than 1,860 miles (3,000 km) from north to south, and cover over 20 degrees of latitude. The four main islands are Honshu, Hokkaido, Kyushu, and Shikoku.

> **WORLD'S RICHEST NATION – JAPAN IS NUMBER ONE**

> **MIRACLE ECONOMY STARTS TO FALTER**

> **DECLINING BIRTH RATE LEADS TO GRAYING POPULATION**

Population	124 million
Area	145,856 sq mi (378,847 sq km)
Currency	Yen
Capital	Tokyo

These Japanese-made vehicles are ready to be loaded onto ships in the port of Yokohama, for export around the world.

Pacific links

Much of Japan's importance as a superpower and trading nation is connected with its location. In the past, there were advantages in being close to China. Japan benefited from China's early development, adopting both the Chinese writing system and style of government. Later, trading links developed between the two countries. Increasingly, Japan is benefiting from links with other countries in the Pacific region. These include many of the world's most powerful and fast-growing economies – the United States, Australia, and the newly industrializing countries of Southeast Asia.

The old and the new

We usually think of Japan as a very modern country, with high-tech factories making advanced electronic goods, large and bustling cities, skyscrapers filled with people working in automated offices, and commuters being whisked rapidly between cities on the bullet train. However, there is another, more traditional, side of Japan. Ancient customs and rituals like the tea ceremony are still practiced. Two very old religions – Buddhism and Shinto – play an important part in Japanese daily life, through their rituals and festivals. The unusual blend of old and new is one of the country's most typical features.

Japan lies off the east coast of Asia, in the northwest part of the Pacific Ocean.

Hokkaido

Honshu

ASIA

Kyushu   Shikoku

PACIFIC OCEAN

The Tokyo Stock Exchange (right) is one of the symbols of the modern face of Japan.

The traditional tea ceremony is intended to help people to appreciate beautiful and simple things. It dates from the fifteenth century.

5

The land and the climate

The landscape of Japan has three important physical characteristics. The country is made up of a large number of islands. Over 70 percent of the terrain is mountainous or hilly. And forest covers much of the land area. These three features pose major challenges to the Japanese people. Large parts of the country are quite difficult to develop. Roads and railroad lines have to be built, where possible, to avoid upland areas. Many areas are not suitable for settlement, so more than 90 percent of the land area is thinly populated.

A mountainous land

Although Japan's mountains are not as high as those of the Himalayas (the world's largest mountain system), they are important enough to influence the country's human geography and systems. Population patterns, transport routes, the locations of cities, and the development of industry have all been affected by the existence of large mountainous areas. As a result, most of Japan's economic activity is confined to the narrow coastal strip. Even here, space for building and development is so limited that much land has had to be reclaimed from the sea.

Mountains cover more than three-quarters of the Japanese landscape. A long coastline is another of the country's important physical features.

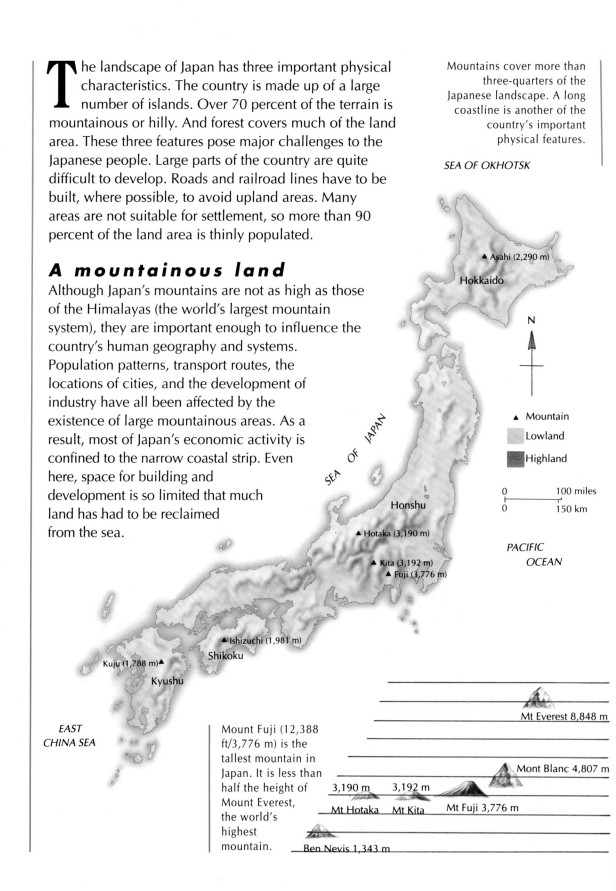

SEA OF OKHOTSK

▲ Asahi (2,290 m)

Hokkaido

N

SEA OF JAPAN

Honshu

▲ Hotaka (3,190 m)

▲ Kita (3,192 m)
▲ Fuji (3,776 m)

▲ Ishizuchi (1,981 m)

Shikoku

Kuju (1,788 m) ▲

Kyushu

EAST CHINA SEA

▲ Mountain

Lowland

Highland

0   100 miles
0   150 km

PACIFIC OCEAN

Mount Fuji (12,388 ft/3,776 m) is the tallest mountain in Japan. It is less than half the height of Mount Everest, the world's highest mountain.

Mt Everest 8,848 m

Mont Blanc 4,807 m

3,190 m   3,192 m

Mt Hotaka   Mt Kita   Mt Fuji 3,776 m

Ben Nevis 1,343 m

Each year, the end of the Japanese winter is marked by the appearance of cherry blossoms. This event is eagerly awaited because the Japanese like to celebrate the arrival of spring with flower-viewing parties. Television weather forecasters have fun predicting when the blossoms will bloom in different parts of Japan.

This hot spring (known as White Pond Hell) is in Beppu on the island of Kyushu, the most southerly of Japan's four main islands. The steam from the boiling water turns a blue-white color as it cools.

A temperate climate

In general, Japan's climate is a temperate one. It does vary quite a lot from one region to another, as the country covers such a huge north–south distance. Areas of southern Japan, like Okinawa and Kyushu for example, are much nearer to the equator than parts of Hokkaido. They are therefore quite warm, and tropical plants grow well in these places.

Further north, in Hokkaido, in winter especially, temperatures can fall as low as –3°F (–10°C). Deep snowfalls are common. The Winter Olympics were held in Sapporo, Hokkaido, in 1972. Many parts of Japan's mountainous interior experience severe weather conditions in winter.

In winter, heavy snow in Hokkaido (shown below) attracts many winter sports enthusiasts as well as visitors to the special snow festivals.

Storm damage

From time to time, extreme weather events threaten Japan's population. The islands lie in the path of tropical storms called typhoons, which form over the North Pacific and then sweep toward the mainland of Asia. During the typhoon season, between June and October, the high winds and heavy rains often cause huge waves, rough seas and widespread flooding, especially in the low-lying coastal areas. The storms damage property, crops, and life. Each of Japan's 47 prefectures now has a special plan that is put into operation to reduce flood damage during the typhoon season.

A hazardous land

Japan is located near the boundary of one of the huge plates that make up the Earth's crust. Japan lies in what is known as an "active zone." This means that it is likely to suffer from volcanic eruptions and earthquakes. Both these natural hazards pose a threat to life and property.

Earthquakes

Each year, there are over 1,000 earthquakes in Japan, and many smaller tremors. Most tremors are so small that they are barely noticed. From time to time a serious earthquake occurs. In 1923, over 100,000 people were killed by the Tokyo and Yokohama, or Great Kanto, earthquake. Most of Tokyo and Yokohama were destroyed by the fires that followed the earthquake. More recently, in 1983, over 100 people lost their lives after a serious earthquake in the central Sea of Japan.

1991:

VOLCANIC LAVA POURS FROM MOUNT UNZEN

1993:

NEW 'QUAKE SPARKS TIDAL WAVES ALONG HOKKAIDO COAST

1923:

FIRES SWEEP CITY AFTER HUGE EARTH TREMOR

100,000 FEARED DEAD AS QUAKE ROCKS TOKYO

1923

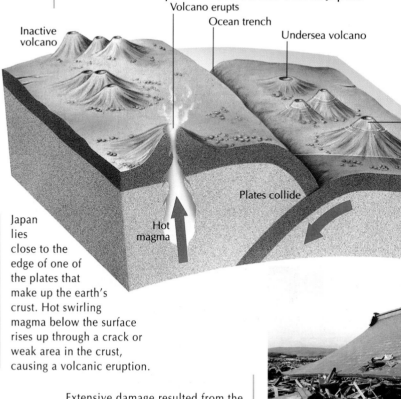

Volcano erupts

Ocean trench

Undersea volcano

Inactive volcano

Volcanic island

Plates collide

Earth's crust

Hot magma

Japan lies close to the edge of one of the plates that make up the earth's crust. Hot swirling magma below the surface rises up through a crack or weak area in the crust, causing a volcanic eruption.

Extensive damage resulted from the earthquake off the coast of Hokkaido on July 12, 1993. Huge tidal waves crashed onto the island, killing local people and destroying many homes.

Volcanic eruptions

Volcanoes are a problem, too. There are over 200 volcanoes dotted around Japan, and at least 50 of these are known to be active today. Mount Fuji, near Tokyo, is perhaps the best-known volcano in Japan, but it has not erupted since 1707. Another volcano, called Mount Unzen, erupted in 1991 on the island of Kyushu, causing the death of 40 people. Most of the dead were scientists who were monitoring the volcano. Late in 1992, Mount Aso, also on Kyushu, started to erupt, but few people were affected because the volcano is situated in a remote area.

New techniques

The Japanese have learned from their experience of volcanoes and earthquakes, and now take steps to prevent serious loss of life and damage to property. They have been developing new techniques for predicting volcanic eruptions and earthquakes. In many areas where there is a risk of these hazards, it is forbidden to build housing, factories, and offices. New skyscrapers in Tokyo and other Japanese cities are built using technology that is designed to withstand the shock of all but the most severe earthquakes.

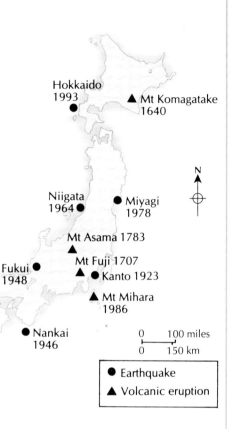

The map shows the location and date of some of Japan's major earthquakes and volcanic eruptions over the past 300 or so years.

Hokkaido 1993
▲ Mt Komagatake 1640

N

Niigata 1964
● Miyagi 1978

Mt Asama 1783 ▲

Fukui ● 1948

Mt Fuji 1707 ▲
● Kanto 1923

▲ Mt Mihara 1986

Mt Unzen ▲ 1792 1991

● Nankai 1946

0   100 miles
0   150 km

● Earthquake
▲ Volcanic eruption

When Mt Unzen erupted on June 3, 1991, clouds of ash and gas billowed up into the air and red-hot lava poured down the mountainside.

Crowded cities, empty countryside

Japan's population has increased steadily during the past 50 or so years, rising from 73 million in 1940 at the start of World War II, to more than 124 million today. This makes Japan the seventh most populous country in the world. However, the rate of population growth has been slowing down since the 1950s. Except for a period of increase during the 1970s, Japan's birthrate is falling.

Japan is a crowded nation. It has a large population and a relatively small land area, so its population density (the number of people per square mile) is greater than that of many other nations. On average, there are about 850 people for every square mile in Japan, compared with 67 in the United States and a world average of 101 people for each square mile. In fact, Japan seems even more crowded, because the majority of the population is concentrated in less than 10 percent of the total land area.

Most people live in towns and cities. Over 50 percent of the total population are in three huge urban areas – Tokyo, Yokohama, and Osaka. Ten of Japan's cities have a population of more than one million.

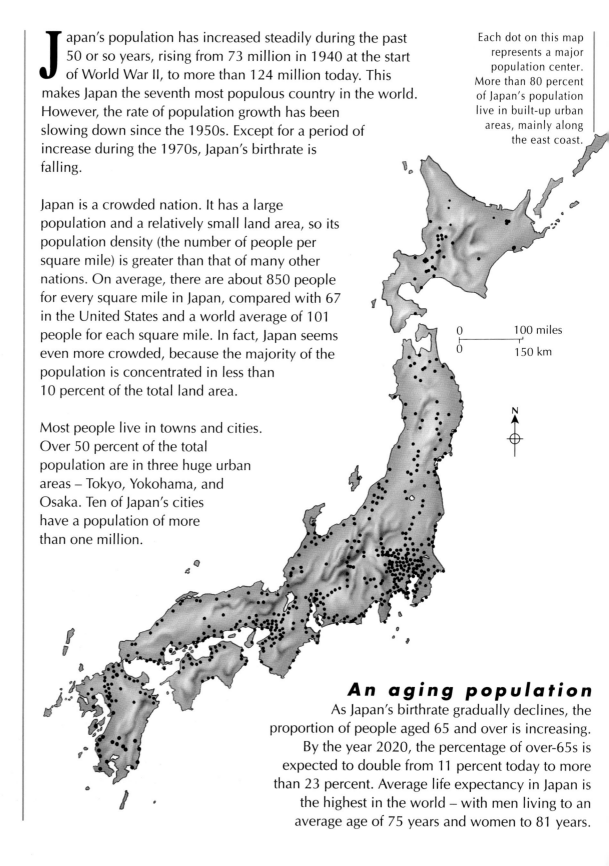

Each dot on this map represents a major population center. More than 80 percent of Japan's population live in built-up urban areas, mainly along the east coast.

0 —— 100 miles
0 —— 150 km

N

An aging population
As Japan's birthrate gradually declines, the proportion of people aged 65 and over is increasing. By the year 2020, the percentage of over-65s is expected to double from 11 percent today to more than 23 percent. Average life expectancy in Japan is the highest in the world – with men living to an average age of 75 years and women to 81 years.

The streets of Tokyo are always crowded. Millions of commuters travel into the city to work each day.

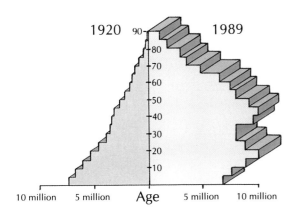

| 1920 | | 1989 |

This pyramid graph shows the age of the Japanese population in 1920 and in 1989. The number of elderly people has increased as people now live to an older age.

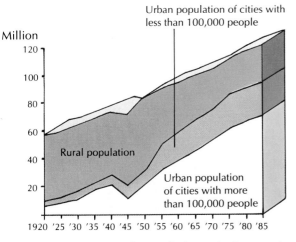

Urban population of cities with less than 100,000 people

Rural population

Urban population of cities with more than 100,000 people

1920 '25 '30 '35 '40 '45 '50 '55 '60 '65 '70 '75 '80 '85

The graph shows the increase in Japan's population between 1920 and 1985.

Although the cities have grown, most Japanese people love the countryside, and spend some leisure time there. A visit to a resort in a remote area, and bathing in its natural spring waters, is a favorite way of spending a weekend away from the city. One of Japan's most popular sports – golf – also takes place in a country setting.

This love of the country may be traced to Shinto, Japan's native religion. According to Shinto, spiritual forces are believed to exist in nature – in the rivers, wind, and the trees. In respect of these spirits the Japanese take care of and enjoy the countryside.

A mixture of peoples

As an island nation, Japan has been influenced by many other nations. The Japanese themselves are descended from a mixture of peoples. Around 18,000 years ago, during the last Ice Age, when sea levels were much lower than today, Japan was physically linked to the mainland of Asia. People are thought to have migrated to Japan. Later, they mixed with people from the Pacific islands and Asia. All these people brought with them their traditions, customs, and language. Since this time, a common language and culture have developed, which unite these various peoples as the race we now recognize as the Japanese.

11

Food, farming, and fishing

The long life expectancy of Japanese people is partly due to their healthy diet. This consists largely of staple crops like rice and beans, and contains a lot of fruit and vegetables. Rice may be eaten with every meal. On average, each person eats 150 pounds (70 kg) of rice in a year.

Japan is almost self-sufficient in food, producing 70 percent of its food requirements. About two-thirds of the fruit and vegetables needed, much of the meat and dairy produce, and all the rice required are actually produced in Japan. A journey through the Japanese countryside shows the importance of rice. It accounts for just under one-third of all farm output.

The two pie charts compare a breakdown of the diet of people in Japan (top) and in the United Kingdom (bottom).

The map shows the different amounts of rice grown each year in different parts of Japan. The highest level of rice production is in the prefectures on the northern island of Hokkaido.

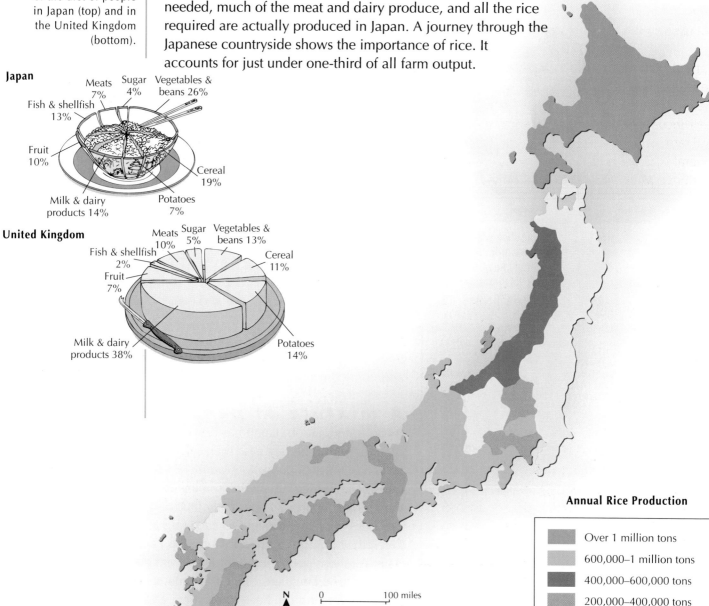

Japan

Meats 7%
Sugar 4%
Vegetables & beans 26%
Fish & shellfish 13%
Fruit 10%
Cereal 19%
Milk & dairy products 14%
Potatoes 7%

United Kingdom

Meats 10%
Sugar 5%
Vegetables & beans 13%
Fish & shellfish 2%
Fruit 7%
Cereal 11%
Milk & dairy products 38%
Potatoes 14%

N

0   100 miles
0   150 km

Annual Rice Production

Over 1 million tons

600,000–1 million tons

400,000–600,000 tons

200,000–400,000 tons

Under 200,000 tons

Intensive farming

Only about 15 percent of Japan's land area can be farmed. As good farmland is in short supply, farms tend to be small. The average farm size is just 2.4 acres (1 hectare), compared with 450 acres (188 h) in the United States. Land has to be used as economically as possible, and so it is farmed intensively. Every effort is made to produce as much as possible from even the smallest plots. To achieve this output, large amounts of fertilizer are used, and as many tasks as possible are mechanized.

This Japanese farmer in Hokkaido is planting rice seedlings by machine.

Agriculture in Japan is organized in a very different way from that of many other developed countries. The small farms rely on family members for their labor. There are over 4 million farm households in Japan, but less than 25 percent earn most of their income from farming. Many farmers may have full-time jobs in offices or stores, and farm only on weekends. During "golden week" in early May each year, there are several national holidays in Japan. Farmers can till their fields and transplant rice seedlings while taking a break from their regular job.

Agricultural land is valuable in Japan because it is in such short supply. Farmers must make use of every part of their land to obtain the maximum amount of produce from it.

The fishing industry

As Japan is surrounded by water, fishing has for a long time provided income for many coastal communities. There are more than 400,000 people working in the fishing industry, and over 170,000 registered fishing vessels in Japan. Fish is an important source of protein in the Japanese diet, and features in many traditional dishes. Sometimes it is served raw in thin strips (*sushi* or *sashimi*) or deep fried with vegetables *(tempura)*. Recently meat has become more popular, and is replacing fish as a major source of protein. Today the fishing industry is in decline, although the annual catch of around 12 million tons is still one of the largest in the world.

The Tsukiji wholesale fish market is in the heart of Japan's capital, Tokyo. Raw and cooked fish are the main ingredients of many different Japanese dishes.

Resources and energy

Although Japan has a wide variety of minerals, it does not have the quantity of minerals that is usually needed to develop manufacturing industries. Basic reserves of most mineral and energy resources are almost entirely lacking in Japan. There are small quantities of iron ore, and only very small coal and oil deposits. Because of this lack of resources, most of the raw materials used by industry and most of Japan's energy supplies must be imported.

These oil tankers are offloading their cargo of crude oil at a terminal in Kagoshima, Kyushu.

Importing raw materials

Importing raw materials and energy supplies is expensive. In order to pay for these imports, Japan exports manufactured goods. High levels of imports also mean that Japan is very dependent on the rest of the world for these resources. Supplies are liable to be interrupted by events that are beyond Japanese control. A war in the Middle East, for example, can interrupt Japan's vital oil supplies. In addition, prices of raw materials and energy supplies may change, even from one day to the next.

Japan is almost unique among the world's developed countries in having such strong manufacturing industries but so few resources. Coal and oil deposits have been almost completely used up, and around 90 percent of primary energy sources must be imported. Imported coal is used extensively in the steel industry, but oil is the most widely used fuel – in factories, homes, and farms and for transportation.

The diagram below shows the value of raw materials, excluding fuels, imported by the United States, Germany, the United Kingdom and Japan in 1990. Japan spent much more on imported raw materials than the other three countries.

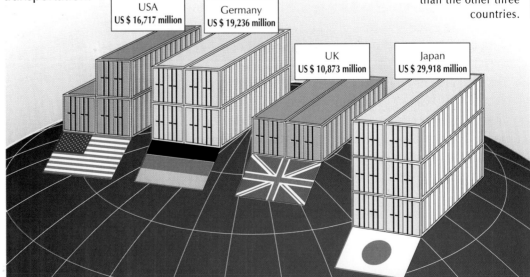

USA
US $ 16,717 million

Germany
US $ 19,236 million

UK
US $ 10,873 million

Japan
US $ 29,918 million

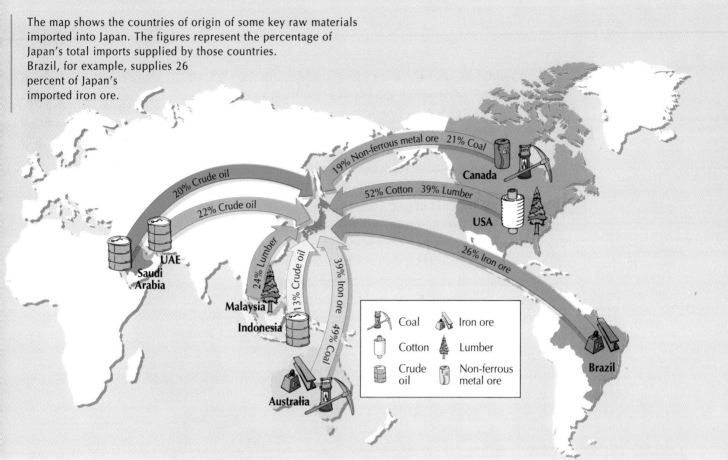

The map shows the countries of origin of some key raw materials imported into Japan. The figures represent the percentage of Japan's total imports supplied by those countries. Brazil, for example, supplies 26 percent of Japan's imported iron ore.

19% Non-ferrous metal ore   21% Coal   Canada

20% Crude oil

22% Crude oil

52% Cotton   39% Lumber   USA

26% Iron ore

24% Lumber

13% Crude oil

39% Iron ore

49% Coal

UAE
Saudi Arabia

Malaysia

Indonesia

Australia

Brazil

Coal		Iron ore	
Cotton		Lumber	
Crude oil		Non-ferrous metal ore	

The consumption of energy per person in Japan is lower than might be expected. A number of campaigns have encouraged people and industries to save energy, so that the nation is not so heavily dependent on imported supplies. Despite this low energy consumption, and perhaps looking ahead to the future, the government has decided to expand Japan's nuclear power capacity. Today, Japan has over 40 nuclear plants, and 10 new facilities are currently being built.

Alternative energy

Alternative forms of energy, using renewable resources, are now being developed. Here, the country's geography provides new opportunities. The earth's crust under Japan is thin and fractured. In some parts of the country, large reservoirs of very hot water lie just beneath the surface. The hot water and steam can be tapped to generate electricity. This kind of renewable energy is called geothermal energy.

The hilly landscape and year-round rainfall in most of Japan mean that many rivers flow quickly. The enormous power of these rivers can be harnessed to produce hydroelectricity. In the future, these alternative energies will become even more important.

Alternative energy sources such as wind power are also being developed in Japan. This wind farm at Tohoku is part of an electricity power plant complex.

Cars, cameras, and chips

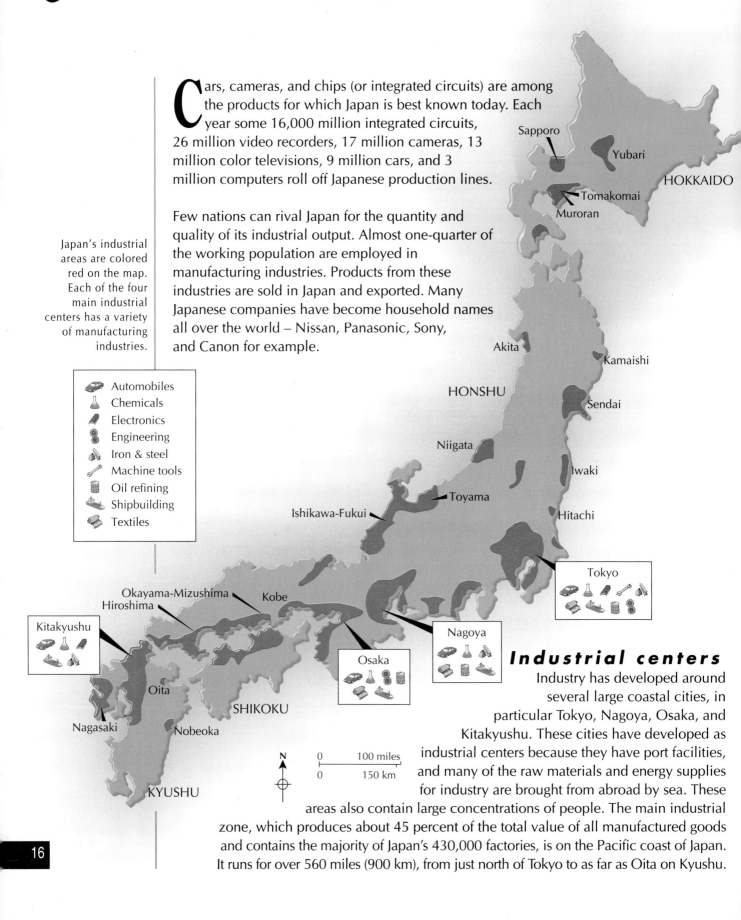

Cars, cameras, and chips (or integrated circuits) are among the products for which Japan is best known today. Each year some 16,000 million integrated circuits, 26 million video recorders, 17 million cameras, 13 million color televisions, 9 million cars, and 3 million computers roll off Japanese production lines.

Few nations can rival Japan for the quantity and quality of its industrial output. Almost one-quarter of the working population are employed in manufacturing industries. Products from these industries are sold in Japan and exported. Many Japanese companies have become household names all over the world – Nissan, Panasonic, Sony, and Canon for example.

Japan's industrial areas are colored red on the map. Each of the four main industrial centers has a variety of manufacturing industries.

Key:
- Automobiles
- Chemicals
- Electronics
- Engineering
- Iron & steel
- Machine tools
- Oil refining
- Shipbuilding
- Textiles

HOKKAIDO

Sapporo
Yubari
Tomakomai
Muroran

HONSHU

Akita
Kamaishi
Sendai
Niigata
Iwaki
Toyama
Ishikawa-Fukui
Hitachi

Tokyo

Okayama-Mizushima
Hiroshima
Kobe
Nagoya
Osaka

Kitakyushu

Oita

SHIKOKU

Nagasaki
Nobeoka

KYUSHU

0   100 miles
0   150 km

Industrial centers

Industry has developed around several large coastal cities, in particular Tokyo, Nagoya, Osaka, and Kitakyushu. These cities have developed as industrial centers because they have port facilities, and many of the raw materials and energy supplies for industry are brought from abroad by sea. These areas also contain large concentrations of people. The main industrial zone, which produces about 45 percent of the total value of all manufactured goods and contains the majority of Japan's 430,000 factories, is on the Pacific coast of Japan. It runs for over 560 miles (900 km), from just north of Tokyo to as far as Oita on Kyushu.

Expanding industry

Following Japan's defeat at the end of World War II, much of Japanese industry was in ruins. Apart from the people, there were few resources with which to develop a strong manufacturing industry.

In the 1960s, the steel, cement-making, and petrochemical industries grew rapidly. Mass production methods were adopted, and huge amounts of energy and other raw materials were imported to keep industry growing. Steel production grew from 2 million tons in 1945 to 100 million tons by the early 1970s. As heavy industries began to face higher costs, they were replaced by newer industries that produced high-value goods. Car production expanded and the electronics industry grew, thanks to advances in microelectronics technology.

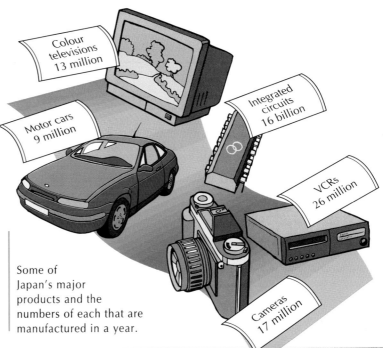

Some of Japan's major products and the numbers of each that are manufactured in a year.

Colour televisions 13 million

Motor cars 9 million

Integrated circuits 16 billion

VCRs 26 million

Cameras 17 million

Daily exercise is a routine part of the working day for many Japanese employees, like these workers in the port of Yokohama.

A job for life

Workers in Japan, whether in factories or offices, change jobs very rarely. A system called "lifetime employment" is still widespread. It means that many workers stay with the same company from the time they leave school until they retire. Although they work long hours and take few vacations, they receive many benefits. Companies take care of their employees and their families, often providing them with housing as well as medical and educational facilities.

Modern assembly lines like the one above are commonplace throughout the Japanese electronics industry.

Getting around

It's not easy to build transportation links in a country made up of thousands of islands, and where much of the landscape is very hilly. But, in fact, it is easier to travel around Japan than might seem likely from a look at its physical geography. Most of the transport routes run north–south along the flatter land near the coast. There are few east–west links, as these would have to cross the mountainous areas.

Transportation around Japan is possible by air, rail, road, and sea. Rail transportation is especially well developed, and there is also an extensive road system of over 625,000 miles (1 million km). Road transportation is less popular than in many countries because it takes longer than rail travel and is less comfortable. Also, cars use expensive imported petroleum and cause more damage to the environment. Despite a rapid increase in the number of cars to around 35 million, many people prefer to take the train, or even to fly.

A network of express road and rail routes links Japan's principal cities and towns. The country has over 70 airports, including the two international ones of Tokyo and Osaka.

Wakkanai

HOKKAIDO

Sapporo

Hakodate

Seikan Tunnel

Aomori

Akita

Morioka

N

0   100 miles
0   150 km

Niigata

HONSHU

Toyama

Tokyo

Yokohama

Nagoya

Seto Ohashi Bridge

Kyoto

Kobe

Osaka

Hiroshima

Kanmon Bridge

Kitakyushu

Fukuoka

Nagasaki

Kumamoto

SHIKOKU

KYUSHU

Kagoshima

⎯⎯	Expressways
⎯✈⎯	Bullet train routes
✈	Airports

Island links

The quickest way to travel between the main islands is by air. Japan has over 70 local airports served by three main airlines. There are also regular ferry services as well as several other links between the main islands. The Seto Ohashi Bridge links Honshu with Shikoku across the Inland Sea. The 34-mile (54-km)-long Seikan Tunnel – the world's longest – links Honshu with Hokkaido. Both were opened in 1988. The Kanmon Bridge and railroad tunnel carry cars and trains south from Honshu to Kyushu.

The amount of freight carried by different transport methods in Japan in one year. More than three-quarters of the goods that are transported across Japan each year are carried by road.

Air	660,500 tons
Rail	82.8 million tons
Sea	538 million tons
Road	5,746.8 million tons

You can travel by the *Shinkansen*, or bullet train, from Morioka in northern Honshu to Fukuoka in Kyushu. The bullet train is shown here with Mount Fuji in the background.

Travel by train

Rail transportation accounts for 40 percent of Japanese passenger traffic. This figure is higher than in many other countries. The best-known train, the *Shinkansen*, or bullet train, is one of the fastest passenger trains in the world, traveling at speeds of up to 160 miles (255 km) per hour. You can travel almost the entire length of Japan's four main islands by train, from Kagoshima in Kyushu to Wakkanai in northern Hokkaido.

A typical scene in Tokyo's Shinjuku subway during the rush hour.

Trains are heavily used within cities, too. Trains on many lines in central Tokyo get so busy that some stations employ special *oshiya*, or pushers, to cram more people into each car. Many people commute to work by train, and where several train lines converge, as at Tokyo's Shinjuku station, massive crowds can develop. About 4 million people pass through Shinjuku station each day. Bicycles are a popular way for commuters to begin their journey into the city each day. Most railroad stations have massive bicycle parking areas. Bicycles are also widely used by young people going to school.

Business people frequently travel around the country by plane or helicopter. These executives are setting off on a trip combining work and their favorite sport – golf.

19

Trading the world

You are likely to see the label "Made in Japan" on many goods. Japan exports a wide variety of items around the world. Since the 1970s, it has been one of the three largest trading nations, together with the United States and Germany.

Many countries have excellent trading links with Japan. The United States and the European Community (EC) are important customers. The United States accounts for around 29 percent of all exports and provides almost one-quarter of all imports. Some countries located much closer to Japan, like Hong Kong, Indonesia, Korea, Taiwan, and Australia, are also major trading partners.

TRADE SURPLUS REACHES NEW HIGH

EXPORT EARNINGS FROM CARS AND ELECTRONICS SURGE AHEAD

JAPAN DOMINATES WORLD TRADE

These workers are loading electronic goods that have been packed for export.

The graph shows the value of Japan's exports and imports between 1979 and 1991. Since 1981, Japan's exports have been worth more than its imports.

US $million
350,000
300,000
250,000
200,000
150,000
100,000
50,000

Imports
Exports

1979 1980 1981 1982 1983 1984 1985 1986 1987 1988 1989 1990 1991

Japanese companies abroad

Another link between Japan and the wider world is investment. Japanese companies spend huge sums of money each year, expanding their activities into other countries. In 1989, they invested about $67,500 million in other countries. The two countries that have attracted most of this investment over the past four decades are the United States and United Kingdom.

Cars and electronic goods like televisions and video cassette recorders (VCRs) are some of the goods manufactured abroad by Japanese companies. Car companies like Nissan, Toyota, and Honda are large employers in both the United States and the United Kingdom. They introduced into these countries modern working practices that have helped to make the companies so successful in Japan. If present trends continue, by the end of the century Japanese companies could be producing up to one-third of all the cars manufactured in the United States and the United Kingdom.

Today, the value of Japan's imports is mainly accounted for by raw materials and energy supplies. Goods sold as exports range from ships and steel to cameras, VCRs, and personal stereos. Japan's exports are largely manufactured items with a high added-value. As Tokyo is one of the world's major financial centers, banking and financial services are also sold around the world.

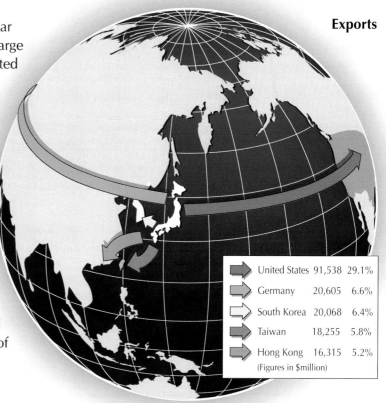

Exports

United States	91,538	29.1%
Germany	20,605	6.6%
South Korea	20,068	6.4%
Taiwan	18,255	5.8%
Hong Kong	16,315	5.2%

(Figures in $million)

The two maps show Japan's five main trading partners for exports (top) and imports (bottom).

United States	53,317	22.5%
China	14,216	6.0%
Australia	13,011	5.5%
Indonesia	12,770	5.4%
South Korea	12,339	5.2%

(Figures in $million)

Imports

A balanced trade?

For more than a decade, Japan has exported far more than it has imported. In this way, Japan makes a huge profit called a trade surplus. Some efforts are now being made to control the level of exports and to increase imports, in order to balance the trading position. Trading links with other nations in the Pacific area are likely to grow, as these countries develop. So Japanese exports seem likely to increase still further.

From isolation to economic superpower

Japan has only recently become a world superpower. The country lay devastated in 1945 at the end of World War II, and since then its economy has been largely rebuilt. However, Japan's history dates back long before World War II.

The islands that make up Japan have been settled for thousands of years. One of the earliest capitals was established at Nara in A.D. 710, before being moved to Kyoto in A.D. 794.

This famous statue of the Great Buddha, completed in 1252, stands in Kamakura, southwest of Tokyo.

With the arrival of Buddhism from China during the sixth century, the music, literature, and painting of that country had a great influence on artistic development in Japan. During the twelfth century, a long period of rule began under a series of shoguns (military rulers). Control of the country was disputed by the various shoguns. Gradually Japan began to look outward, and trade with the Chinese, Portuguese, and Dutch grew. Many missionaries came to Japan, including Saint Francis Xavier, who introduced Christianity during the sixteenth century. However, one of the shoguns regarded these missionaries as a threat, and forbade people to become Christians.

This shogun, or military ruler, is shown in his full battle array.

Isolation from the outside world

In order to assert control over the country, one of the shoguns cut the country off from the outside world in the 1630s. Trips abroad by Japanese people were forbidden in 1635, some foreign ships were not allowed to enter Japanese ports in 1639, and Western books were banned. Two centuries of virtual isolation from the rest of the world began. Throughout this period, Japanese commerce, industry, and the arts all flourished.

This contemporary engraving shows the American naval commander Commodore Perry negotiating his trade agreement with the Japanese authorities.

During this time of isolation, countries like the United States, which had once had strong links with Japan, continued to demand supplies and to seek trade deals. Eventually, Japan was forced to open its doors to the rest of the world. In 1853 Commodore Matthew Perry of the U.S. Navy arrived in Tokyo Bay with a squadron of four warships. As a result, in 1854 a treaty was signed which restarted trade with the United States. Similar treaties were signed with Russia, Britain, the Netherlands, and France.

In the Meiji period (1867–1912), during the reign of Emperor Mutsuhito (who ruled under the name of Meiji), Japan started to modernize. The capital was moved from Kyoto to Edo (modern Tokyo), and a new constitution was passed. Wars were fought and won with China and Russia. Then came the disaster of World War II, following which the Japanese rebuilt their nation to become the economic superpower of today.

The A-Bomb Dome in Hiroshima is the only ruined building that was preserved following the atomic bomb explosion. The building was formerly the city's Industrial Promotion Hall.

Japanese people may be more influenced by western fashion than in the past, but they are at the forefront of developing new technologies as they move towards the next century.

Hiroshima destroyed

One of the most dramatic events in Japan's history occurred at exactly 8.15 A.M. on August 6, 1945. At this moment, the United States Air Force dropped an atomic bomb on the city of Hiroshima. Most of the city was destroyed. Over 100,000 people were killed immediately, and thousands more died later from radiation poisoning. Three days later, another bomb was dropped on Nagasaki. Japan surrendered, and its involvement in World War II ended.

Metropolis Japan

In 1992, Tokyo surpassed Mexico City as the world's most populated urban area. If the populations of all the neighboring densely populated towns and cities are included, then there are over 25 million people living in the Tokyo area. The core of Tokyo city is much smaller, but it still has over 8 million inhabitants.

Many of Japan's largest cities are located along the eastern seaboard. Of the 10 largest urban areas, only Fukuoka faces China. The large cities are not evenly spread, and many are grouped together. These groups of cities are called conurbations. For example, close to Tokyo are the cities of Yokohama and Kawasaki. The country's third largest city, Osaka, lies close to the cities of Kobe and Kyoto.

The Japanese population lives in less than 10 percent of the country's total land area. The metropolis of Tokyo now includes 87 surrounding cities and towns.

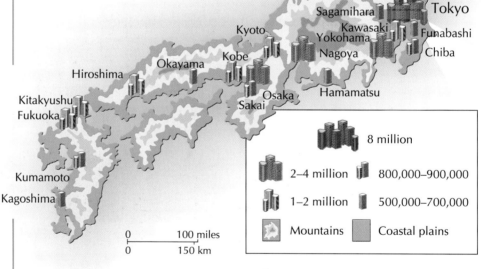

	8 million
2–4 million	800,000–900,000
1–2 million	500,000–700,000
Mountains	Coastal plains

0   100 miles
0   150 km

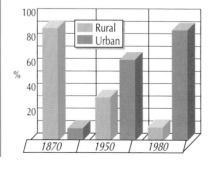

The percentages of Japan's rural and urban populations changed dramatically between 1870 and 1980.

The urban–rural balance

Traditionally, most Japanese people have lived in small villages in the country. For centuries they depended on farming the land and on fishing. Since World War II, the balance between the populations of urban and rural areas has switched in favor of the urban areas. This change began with the expansion of manufacturing industry, which attracted many more people to the urban centers.

24

City life

In many ways, Japanese cities are noisy, bustling places, like cities in other parts of the world. Most are very congested and, in the past, have suffered from serious pollution. A mixture of old and new buildings is quite typical. Houses in Japan are traditionally quite small. In many cities, small two-story wooden houses can be found beside tall new *danchi*, or apartment houses.

In the city centers, large numbers of stores and services compete for space with factories and office buildings. The result is that there are many underground shopping areas in the large cities. These are often linked to busy train stations. Every spare piece of land is used. Tall buildings are common because the land prices in city centers are so high – gardens or even golf driving ranges are commonly found on the tops of these buildings.

Padded mattresses called futons are seen here on the balconies of a modern apartment building in Tokyo. To the left of the building are some examples of more traditional Japanese housing.

A wide range of industrial and commercial activities takes place in the main districts of Tokyo's centre.

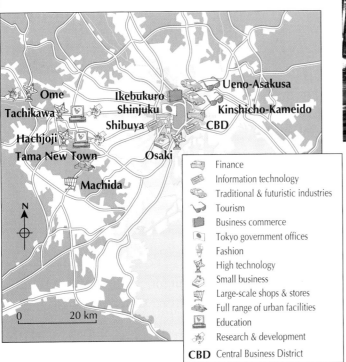

Ome
Tachikawa
Ikebukuro
Shinjuku
Ueno-Asakusa
Shibuya
Kinshicho-Kameido
Hachjoji
CBD
Tama New Town
Osaki
Machida
N

0   20 km

Finance
Information technology
Traditional & futuristic industries
Tourism
Business commerce
Tokyo government offices
Fashion
High technology
Small business
Large-scale shops & stores
Full range of urban facilities
Education
Research & development
CBD Central Business District

Main streets in the cities are very broad, and store signs and street names, which are often missing, are written in Japanese characters. At night the cities take on a special feel. The tall buildings have huge advertising billboards sitting on top of them, which light up brightly.

The lights of downtown Tokyo shine with dazzling brightness at night.

Environment under threat

Japan's rapid economic growth has had serious consequences for the environment. In the postwar years, large quantities of coal and oil were consumed in Japan's booming smelters, steel mills, and factories. The burning of these fuels produced air pollutants like soot, dust, and sulfur and nitrogen oxides. As most industries were located close to densely populated communities, many people were exposed to air pollution.

The problems caused by Japan's dash for economic growth seriously affected both air and water quality. The air in many Japanese cities was so dangerous to breathe that people began to wear face masks. Tokyo Bay, the Inland Sea, and many rivers became polluted.

Electronic pollution scoreboards like the one below give information about the levels of air pollution in Japanese cities.

The Kushiro Shitsugen National Park is situated on the island of Hokkaido.

A cleaner environment

Much has now been done to improve Japan's environment. Sulfur emissions into the air are controlled, all new cars are fitted with catalytic converters to reduce the output of carbon monoxide, and lead-free gasoline has been introduced. Discharges into rivers of waste that contains toxic metals like cadmium and mercury are strictly regulated. Large areas of countryside have been declared protected zones and national parks. The Inland Sea and Tokyo Bay are now much cleaner. Even at home the Japanese are doing their bit for the environment, and many recycling programs are now well developed.

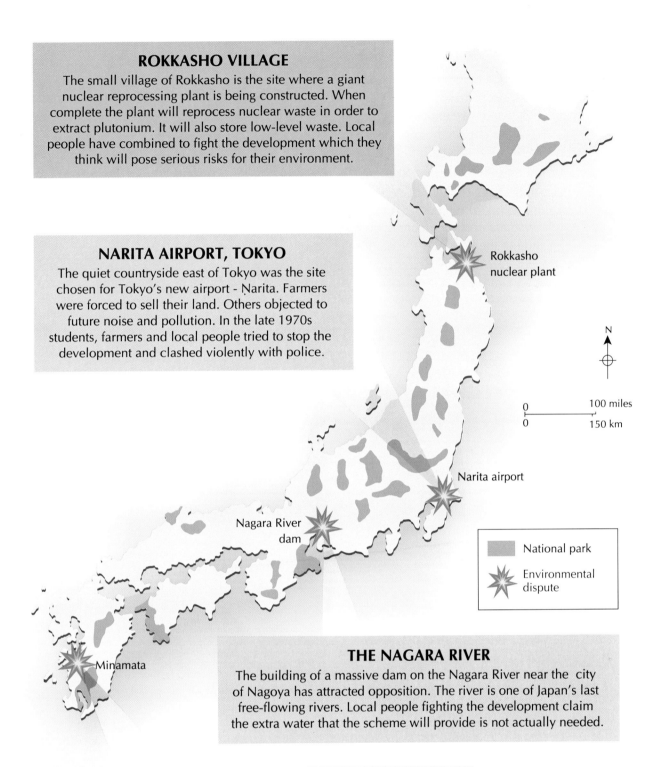

ROKKASHO VILLAGE

The small village of Rokkasho is the site where a giant nuclear reprocessing plant is being constructed. When complete the plant will reprocess nuclear waste in order to extract plutonium. It will also store low-level waste. Local people have combined to fight the development which they think will pose serious risks for their environment.

NARITA AIRPORT, TOKYO

The quiet countryside east of Tokyo was the site chosen for Tokyo's new airport - Narita. Farmers were forced to sell their land. Others objected to future noise and pollution. In the late 1970s students, farmers and local people tried to stop the development and clashed violently with police.

Rokkasho nuclear plant

N

| 0 | 100 miles |
| 0 | 150 km |

Narita airport

Nagara River dam

| National park |
| Environmental dispute |

Minamata

THE NAGARA RIVER

The building of a massive dam on the Nagara River near the city of Nagoya has attracted opposition. The river is one of Japan's last free-flowing rivers. Local people fighting the development claim the extra water that the scheme will provide is not actually needed.

MINAMATA DISEASE

Dead fish and birds were the first signs that the waters of Minamata Bay were badly polluted. In 1956 several local people became seriously ill. The Chisso Corporation, a chemical company, had allowed mercury to leak into the river. This contaminated fish in the river and people eating this fish were also affected. The sickness was known as Minamata Disease. Over 350 people died from it, and thousands were crippled.

Power in the Pacific

A massive expansion of economic activity is taking place in the Pacific region. Japan is already an economic superpower, but many other nations located around the edges of this vast ocean are developing rapidly. Taiwan, Singapore, Thailand, Korea, and Hong Kong have all achieved high growth rates in the past decade, and the economies of Australia and China are becoming stronger. On the other side of the Pacific is the giant economy of the United States.

The economies of many of the countries around the Pacific Rim are growing rapidly. Japan lies at the very heart of this area of economic strength and power.

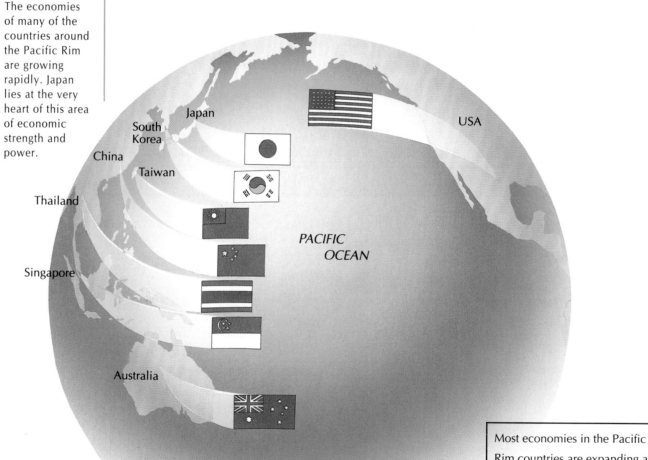

Japan
South Korea
China
Taiwan
Thailand
Singapore
Australia
USA
PACIFIC OCEAN

Most economies in the Pacific Rim countries are expanding at rates of over 5 percent a year. Labor costs in these countries are low, and manufacturing industry is spreading rapidly. It seems likely that more trading links and increased cooperation will lead, in future decades, to the Pacific Rim becoming the powerhouse of the world.

Problems

Some criticism from abroad has been directed at the support that the Japanese government gives to industries. The Ministry of International Trade and Industry (MITI) does offer advice and support to industries, and invests in research and development, especially in new technology. Some countries object to this form of aid, and believe that it gives Japanese companies an unfair advantage.

A trade surplus

At present, many countries spend large amounts of money buying Japanese goods, but face difficulties when they try to sell their own goods to Japan. They accuse Japan of "protecting" its own industries. This is especially true of farm products. Although Japan is one of the world's biggest spenders on food imports, foreign companies often find it difficult to export their goods to Japan. Rice imports are actually banned. If Japan is going to reduce its huge trade surplus, more goods must be allowed into the country. The level of Japanese exports must also be lowered. Without a reduction of the trade surplus, there could be a serious trade war between Japan and countries such as the United States and the European Community. The Japanese have now committed themselves to reducing this surplus.

Japan's space program is organized by NASDA (National Space Development Agency of Japan). NASDA has already launched many artificial satellites, including weather-forecasting, telecommunications, and broadcasting ones.

Keeping ahead

Continuous developments in transport, biotechnology, fiber optics, and integrated circuit technology should ensure that Japan has the lead in producing new products. Japan already has more industrial robots than any other country. In transport, too, new technology is being pioneered to develop a high-speed "maglev" train ("maglev" is short for magnetic levitation). The Japanese are working hard to ensure that they stay ahead of their competitors – both in neighboring countries and in other parts of the world.

The "maglev" train seen here is a prototype. When developed, the train will be even faster than the *Shinkansen*, and may run at speeds of up to 215 miles (350 km) per hour.

Databank

Population

- The population density of Japan – 850 people per square mile – is the 12th highest in the world.
- Overcrowding is a fact of life in Japan — the cities are among the most crowded in the world.
- The situation is no better even when people die. For every place in the Tokyo cemetery there are an average of 12 applicants.
- The five most popular family names in Japan are: Sato, Suzuki, Takahashi, Tanaka, and Watanabe.
- Japanese people are traveling abroad in larger numbers than ever before. In 1990, some 10 million Japanese visited foreign countries.

Physical geography

- The highest temperature ever recorded in Japan is 105°F (40.8°C) in Yamagata Prefecture in 1933.
- The lowest temperature ever recorded is –40°F (–41°C) in Hokkaido in 1902.
- Japan's largest lake, Lake Biwa, has a surface area of 265 square miles (670 sq km) and a maximum depth of 340 feet (103.8 m).
- The Marunouchi business district and Ginza shopping area, in the heart of Tokyo, are built on land that was reclaimed from the sea over three centuries ago.

Food and drink

- One-third of all the tuna fish caught in the world is eaten by the Japanese.
- Until the twelfth century, records show that the Japanese only had two meals each day – one in the early morning and one in the evening.
- A Japanese-style breakfast is a full meal consisting of boiled rice, *nori* (dried seaweed), *miso* (a thick soup), and *tsukemono* (pickles).
- *Saké* is Japan's national drink. It is made from rice, using a brewing process which gives it an alcoholic content of about 15 percent – a little stronger than most wine. *Saké* is usually served warm in small cups.
- Many office workers eat lunch from a lunch box, or *bento*. This usually contains a little raw fish, meat, rice, pickle, and tofu.

Customs

- The average Japanese person works over 250 hours a year more than his or her counterpart elsewhere in the Western world.
- Instead of shaking hands like most Westerners, the Japanese bow. This is called *Ojigi*.
- The depth of the bow depends on who you are greeting: 15° is the correct angle for equals, 30° when meeting superiors and 45° for VIPs or when apologizing.
- Many Japanese streets, even in large cities, have no names.

As a result, some taxi drivers may not know their way around. Police boxes, or *koban*, are used by people asking for directions.

- The *Yomiuri Shimbun*, Japan's leading newspaper, sells over 15 million copies each day.
- Many Japanese customs and traditions, both old and new, are now familiar in other countries, for example origami (paper-folding), karaoke (singing along to a soundtrack played by a machine), sumo (traditional wrestling), and many martial arts.
- Japan has 12 national holidays each year. Many are important festivals:
    Children's Day (May 5)
    Respect for the Aged Day (September 15)
    Shichi-go-san (November 15)
- On *Shichi-go-san*, girls age 3 and 7 years and boys aged 5 are taken to a shrine or temple to pray for good health.
- The Japanese wash themselves with soap before they get into the bathtub. Most tubs are square and quite deep, and the water is very hot.
- According to tradition, you must remove your shoes before entering a Japanese home. Slippers are often provided at the door.
- When you enter a room with a floor of *tatami* (matting made from woven rushes), it is polite to remove even your slippers.

Young people

- Most young people study English at school as their main foreign language, for three years in middle school and for another three years in high school.
- Many young people have difficulty with their English conversation because lessons concentrate on grammar and vocabulary.
- Most school schedules are long, and children rarely return home before the late afternoon. Lessons also take place on Saturday mornings.
- Many children attend private cramming schools, or *juku*, especially to prepare for examinations.
- Lessons in calligraphy are held in every school. By the age of 6, children must know 881 characters. This increases to about 2,000 different characters by the time they leave school.

Political structure

- Japan is a democracy ruled over by a directly elected parliament called the Diet.
- The Diet has two houses: the House of Representatives and the House of Councillors. The Diet has a total of 764 elected members.
- All Japanese people over 20 years of age can vote in elections.
- Japan is divided into 47 prefectures. Each prefecture has an elected government which is responsible for running local services.

Glossary

added-value
When something is cheap to make but can be sold for a much higher price.

catalytic converter
A type of filter that removes the harmful gases from car exhausts.

danchi
Large apartment buildings or complexes.

Earth's crust
The hard outer layer around the earth. Beneath the crust is a mixture of hot liquid rocks and metal.

geothermal energy
The energy produced by water that is heated naturally inside the earth. Steam from the hot water turns turbines that generate geothermal electricity.

golden week
A holiday week in May. Many Japanese farmers take a break from their regular jobs to transplant their rice seedlings.

hydroelectricity
Electricity that is generated by the power of fast-flowing rivers or waterfalls.

integrated circuits
Tiny parts that are fitted inside electronics products.

life expectancy
The average number of years that a person can expect to live.

lifetime employment
The system by which many workers are employed by the same company throughout their working life.

maglev train
A high-speed train under development that is moved along a track by powerful magnets.

nuclear waste
The material that is left after nuclear fuels have been used to generate electricity. It is very dangerous and has to be stored in a safe place.

oshiya
Pushers who are employed to squeeze people into trains.

population density
The average number of people living in a particular area of land.

prefectures
The political units into which Japan is divided for local government purposes (like American states or English counties).

renewable energy
Energy from a source that can be used again and again, such as wind energy.

sashimi
Thin slices of raw fish.

Shinkansen
A high-speed train that travels at speeds of up to 160 mph (255 km/h). It is sometimes called the "bullet train."

Shinto
Japan's native religion.

shogun
A military ruler.

sushi
Mounds of rice topped with raw fish.

tempura
Seafood and vegetables covered in batter and deep fried.

trade surplus
When the value of a country's exports is higher than the value of its imports.

trade war
A dispute between two or more countries about the amount of imported and exported goods.

tremor
A slight shaking of the earth's crust.

typhoon
Severe storms that bring high winds and heavy rain.

Index

agriculture 12–13
air transportation 18, 19, 26

bicycles 19
Buddhism 5, 22

cars 4, 16, 17, 18, 20, 26
China 4, 21, 22, 23, 28
climate 7, 9, 30
coal 14, 15, 26

Diet 30
diet 12, 13

earthquakes 6, 8–9
economy 4, 22, 28–29
electronics industry 16, 17, 20
Emperor Mutsuhito 23
employment 16, 17
energy resources 14, 15, 21
environment 26–27
exports 14, 20, 21, 29

farming 12–13
fishing industry 13
food 12, 28, 30

geothermal energy 15, 31
golden week 13, 31

Hiroshima 23
history 11, 22–23
Hokkaido 4, 7, 8, 13, 16, 18, 27
Honshu 4, 16, 18
hydroelectricity 15, 31

imports 14, 15, 20, 21, 29
industry 16–17, 28, 29
integrated circuits 16, 17
iron ore 14, 15

Kanmon Bridge 18
Kawasaki 24

Kitakyushu 16
Kushiro Shitsugen National Park 26
Kyoto 22, 23, 24
Kyushu 4, 7, 9, 16, 18

Lake Biwa 30
life expectancy 10, 12, 31

maglev train 29, 31
manufacturing industry 14, 16, 24, 28, 29
Meiji period 23
Minamata Bay 27
minerals 6, 14
missionaries 22
mountains 6
Mount Aso 9
Mount Fuji 6, 9
Mount Unzen 9

Nagara River dam 27
Nagasaki 23
Nagoya 16, 24, 27
Narita airport 27
national holidays 13, 30
national parks 26, 27
nuclear power 15, 27, 31

oil 14, 15, 26
Okinawa 7
Osaka 10, 16, 24

Perry, Matthew 23
physical features 6, 7, 8
pollution 25, 26, 27
population 4, 10–11, 24, 30, 31
ports 16
prefectures 7, 13, 30, 31

rail transportation 18, 19, 29
raw materials 14, 15, 21
rice 12, 13, 29
road transportation 18, 19

school 30
Seikan Tunnel 18
Seto Ohashi Bridge 18
Shikoku 4, 16, 18
Shinjuku Station 19
Shinkansen 18, 19, 31
Shinto 5, 11, 31
shogun 22, 31
steel industry 14, 16, 17

tea ceremony 5
Tokyo 11, 16, 19, 21, 25, 30
    population 10, 24
Tokyo earthquake (1923) 8
Tokyo Stock Exchange 5
trade 4, 20–21, 22, 23
trade surplus 20, 21, 29, 31
transportation 18–19, 29
typhoons 7, 31

volcanoes 6, 8, 9

World War II 23

Yokohama 4, 8, 10, 24